Enemies
of the
Secret Hide-out

Story and pictures

by JOHN PETERSON

SCHOLASTIC BOOK SERVICES
NEW YORK · TORONTO · LONDON · AUCKLAND · SYDNEY · TOKYO

To Joey, who loves the woods

Contents

The New Members

"SIGN YOUR NAME RIGHT THERE," said Matt Burns. "Sign it in red ink. Then you'll be a junior member of the Viking Club."

"We use red ink because it looks like blood," said Sam. Sam was Matt's younger brother.

The new boy bent over the paper and signed it.

"Hey! You signed your name Russell!" said Beany. "I thought your name was Rusty."

"Hey, Matt!" said Rusty. He pointed to Beany. "Is this nosy little kid a member of the club too?"

"Sure," said Matt. "Beany is a *senior* member, just like my brother and me."

"I thought your name was Rusty," said Beany again.

"So what!" said Rusty. "Don't you know the difference between a nickname and a real name? Anyway I'd rather be called *anything* than a silly name like Beany."

"*I* don't think Beany is a silly name," said Sam. He walked over and stood between Rusty and Beany. "Besides — pick on somebody your own size. Beany is two years younger than you."

"I was only joking," said Rusty. "Can't you guys take a joke?"

"All right, everybody. Let's stop fighting about nothing," said Matt. "We've got work to do."

"What do we do next?" said Rusty. "Do I get to see the secret hide-out now?"

"Not yet," said Matt. "First, as president of the Viking Club, it is my duty to tell you that you are now a junior member. If you can pass the tests, you'll get to be a senior member like Sam, Beany, and me. Then we'll show you where the secret hide-out is."

"What tests?" said Rusty. "Did all you guys take the tests? Or is this something you're going to make me do because I'm new in the neighborhood?"

"Are you kidding?" said Sam. "Me and my brother are new around here too. We're just staying with our Grandma Burns during summer vacation."

"We all took the tests," said Matt.

"And *passed* them," said Sam.

"Even Beany?" asked Rusty.

"Sure," said Sam. "How do you think he got to be a senior member?"

"You see," said Matt, "the Viking Club has this secret book with all the rules and signals. And the book has four tests you have to pass before you can be a senior member. After you pass the tests, we all go to the secret hide-out, and you can take the oath of membership."

"You put your hand on the secret book and swear never to tell where the secret hide-out is," said Sam.

"Wait until you see the secret hide-out, Rusty," said Beany. "It's keen."

"How about the two kids next door to me?" said Rusty. "Can they join too?"

"You mean those Pelton twins, Larry and Harry?" asked Sam.

"They can join next time we get new members," said Matt. "All of us old members agreed to enroll two kids at a time. After you become a member, we can ask the Peltons."

"You said *two* guys," said Rusty. "Who's the other one besides me?"

"His name is Ted," said Matt. "He lives over on Greene Avenue. Beany and Ted are in the same class in school."

"Oh, another baby," said Rusty. "Ha-ha! When do we take the tests?"

"You can take some of them this afternoon," said Matt. "Ted will be here then. You can take them together."

"There's a high jump that's awfully hard to make," said Beany. "Are you a good jumper?"

"Don't worry about me, kid," said Rusty. "I can do anything a fat little boy like you can do." He patted Beany on the head. "I'll see you guys later. I have to go home and put my sneakers on and eat lunch."

"We'll meet you at two o'clock behind my grandma's house," said Matt. "We'll have everything ready for the tests."

After Rusty left, Sam said, "I don't think Rusty should talk to Beany like that. Beany may be small, but he's still a senior member of the club."

"Well," said Matt, "maybe he meant it in a friendly way. After all, he's new around here. Why should he want any trouble?"

Later that afternoon the Viking Club members were in Grandma Burns's back yard. They were watching Ted take the tests. Rusty came running. He was out of breath.

"Hey, Rusty! You're late," said Matt. "We thought you weren't coming. Ted is doing the tests without you."

"He's been around the course two times already," said Sam. "One more time and he'll pass the obstacle-course test."

"Why didn't you wait? You should have waited," said Rusty. "What do I have to do to catch up?"

"Just follow behind Ted on his last time around," said Matt. "Then run around two more times by yourself."

Rusty ran onto the course behind Ted.

"Come on, Ted!" yelled Beany. "Don't make any mistakes, or you'll have to start over."

"Boy, that's a tough rule," said Sam.

"You've got to have tough tests," said Matt. "Otherwise you don't get good members."

"Come on, Ted!" Beany yelled again. Ted had just zigzagged through some milk cartons without knocking them over. Now he ran toward the last high jump of the test. His shirttail was flying as he leaped.

"Hooray!" yelled Matt. "He made it!"

Matt, Sam, and Beany rushed over to Ted. They shook his hand and patted him on the back.

Ted smiled. "Boy! I'm out of breath." He flopped down on the grass.

"Gee," said Sam. "You were the fastest yet. Faster than Matt, even."

"You can run like anything," said Beany.

"Hey! Look at that," said Sam. He pointed toward the obstacle course. The boys turned and looked. They saw Rusty. He was running past the milk cartons. He wasn't zigzagging between them.

"Hey, Rusty! Hold it! Stop!" Matt shouted. He ran over to where Rusty was standing.

"What's wrong?" said Rusty. "Why did you stop me? I was just getting going."

"You didn't zigzag," said Matt. "You ran past the milk cartons. That's not the right way to do it."

"Aw, so what?" said Rusty. "You saw me zigzag between them the first time. What's the difference? You know I can do it."

"But you have to do it *three* times without a mistake. Just like all of us did," said Matt.

"Why don't we give him another chance?" said Beany.

"I don't want any help from you, baby Beany," said Rusty. "I don't want to be in your dumb club anyway. I have more important things to do." He walked away.

"Wait a minute," Matt called. But Rusty kept on going.

"Boy!" said Sam. "Are we lucky he didn't get in the club. He's coo-coo."

"I wonder what makes him act that way," said Matt.

"What's the next test?" said Ted. "I hope it's more running. I could run all day long."

A Message

THE NEXT AFTERNOON Matt, Sam, and Beany were waiting for Ted. They were in Grandma Burns's yard. They were lying in the grass under the shade of the oak tree.

"As soon as Ted gets here, we'll head for the secret hide-out," said Matt.

"Why is he so late?" said Beany.

"He's looking for the secret hide-out," said Matt.

"What for?" said Beany. "I thought we were going to show him where it is."

"Matt thought it would be a good idea if Ted tried to find the hide-out," said Sam. "Then we'd know if it was really hard to find."

"He'll never find it," said Beany. "Not in a million years."

Just then a paper airplane came sailing over the bush near the fence. It landed next to Beany's feet.

"Who threw that?" Matt stood up and looked toward the fence.

"Hey! Who's that tall, skinny kid running away?" said Sam. "Is it Larry Pelton?" He jumped up and ran over to the fence. "It looked like one of the Pelton twins, didn't it?"

"I don't know," said Matt. "I didn't get a good look at him."

"Look at this, you guys!" shouted Beany. He opened the paper airplane and smoothed out the wrinkles. "There's a message on this paper."

All three boys tried to read the message out loud at the same time.

"Stop it!" said Matt. "I can't hear myself think. Why doesn't one person read it?"

Beany handed the message to Matt. "Here, you read it. You're the president."

Matt read the message aloud: *To the Viking Club — We are going to do something terrible to*

To the Viking Club—
We are going to do
something terrible to
your club very soon.
You can't do anything
to stop us.

your club very soon. You can't do anything to
stop us.

"Who signed it?" said Sam.

"Nobody," said Matt. "There's a drawing of a
death's head at the bottom."

"Death's head!" said Beany. "What's that?"

"Golly, Beany," said Sam. "Don't you know anything? It's a skull and crossbones like the pirates
used."

"It means danger," said Matt. "Whoever sent the
message means to do something terrible all right.
If it really was one of the Pelton twins, why would
he want to do that? We aren't their enemies."

"You forgot about Rusty," said Sam. "He's their friend. And he was really sore yesterday when we caught him cheating. I'll bet it was Rusty and the Pelton twins."

"I wish I knew," said Matt.

"Hey!" said Beany. "Why don't we see if the handwriting on the message is the same as Rusty's handwriting?"

"That's a great idea, Beany," said Matt. "He signed his name in red ink, remember?"

"I'll get the paper," said Sam. "It's in our room with the secret book and everything." He ran into the house. In a few minutes he was back with the paper.

"Look at that!" said Matt. "It's the same handwriting. See how he makes the L's — they have big round loops."

"And see how he makes the U," said Sam. "It looks just like a V."

Just then Ted came into the yard. He sat down under the tree and leaned against the trunk. "I give up," he said. "I looked all over the woods where you told me to look, and I didn't see anything. That secret hide-out is really a secret."

"Look at this message," said Matt. He handed the paper airplane message to Ted.

"Holy cats!" said Ted. "Who wrote this?"

"We think Rusty did," said Matt.

"You know what?" said Ted. "I saw Rusty with one of those Pelton kids in the woods just now. They were fixing up that old tree house — the one near the cow path."

"Hey, Matt," said Sam. "You know what that means, don't you?"

"I bet Rusty started a club of his own," said Matt, "and he wants to get even with us. We'd better sneak over there tonight and take a look around."

"What for?" said Beany.

"We have to protect ourselves, that's why," said Matt. "Maybe we can find out what their plans are."

"Do we have to go at night?" Beany wanted to know.

"Golly, Beany! You're always asking such silly questions," said Sam.

"If it's dark, they probably won't see us," said Matt. "Let's meet back here after supper. And everyone bring a flashlight. O.K?"

"When do I get to see the secret hide-out?" said Ted.

"Tonight," said Matt. "We'll go to the secret hide-out for a meeting right after we spy on Rusty's clubhouse."

A Dark Night

IT WAS ALMOST DARK when the boys met again under the oak tree.

"Is everyone here?" said Matt.

They looked at one another and nodded.

"I'm not supposed to stay out too late," said Beany.

"Look, Beany," said Sam. "If you're scared, just say so. We can go without you."

"Who's scared?" said Beany. "I'm not scared any more than you are."

"Let's not fight with each other," said Matt. "Let's worry about Rusty and his gang instead."

"How many guys does he have in his club?" said Beany.

"That's one of the things we have to find out," said Matt. "Did you all bring flashlights?"

"Everyone has a flashlight," said Ted.

"O.K.," said Matt. "Then let's go."

The boys started off to find the tree house. They climbed over the fence near the woods.

"Keep your flashlights turned off," said Matt, "or they'll see us coming."

"Boy, these woods sure are dark," said Beany.

"I can't see anything," said Ted. "Where's the path?"

"Just stand here for a minute," said Matt, "and your eyes will get used to the dark."

They waited. Soon they could see the shapes of the trees and bushes.

"There it is," said Matt. "There's the path. Let's go." He walked into the woods. Ted and Sam followed him.

"Hey!" said Beany. "Wait for me!" He ran to catch up with his friends.

Soon they were deep in the woods. The moonlight shone through the trees. It made spooky shadows on the path.

Suddenly they heard a quick flapping noise. Then the air was full of flying things. They darted back and forth in front of the boys.

"Watch out!" said Sam.

"What's that?" said Beany. He covered his head with his arms.

"Bats!" said Matt. "There's a hollow tree nearby. They won't bump into you. Bats are the best flyers in the world."

"I thought it was an ambush," said Beany.

"You know, Beany," said Sam, "for the first time I have to agree with you."

"There's the tree house," said Matt. Everybody stopped.

The boys looked into the darkness. They saw a black, boxlike shape in a tree just ahead.

"Are we all going over there?" Beany whispered.

"No," said Matt. "I have a plan. Listen." The boys gathered around him. "We'll draw straws to see who goes. The person with the shortest straw will sneak over first. He'll see if anyone's there. The rest of us

will surround the place. If there's trouble, we can
charge in and surprise them. Then we'll get away.
Afterward we'll all meet at the secret hide-out.
O.K.?"

"What about me?" said Ted. "How am I going to
get to the secret hide-out? I don't even know where
it is."

"Stick with me," said Matt. "No matter what
happens — stick with me."

"How do we draw straws?" said Beany.

"Watch," said Matt, "and you'll see."

Matt broke off four small sticks from a dried twig. He made three of them the same size. He made the fourth one smaller than the others. Then he held them in his hand. No one could see which one was the smallest. "Pick one!" he said.

One by one, each boy took a stick from Matt's hand. "Who got the smallest stick?" said Matt.

"I think I did," said Beany.

"Hold it up and let's see," said Matt.

"Wow-ee!" said Sam. "It is! Beany has to go over to the tree house all by himself."

The Tree House

"Now remember, Beany," said Matt. "If you need any help, hold your flashlight up in the air. Then wave it back and forth. And don't forget to light it first."

"O.K.," said Beany. "I'll just sneak over there and look around. Then I'll come right back."

"Hey, Matt!" said Sam. He pulled at Matt's shirtsleeve. "Maybe I'd better go instead. Don't you think Beany's a little small for the job?"

"Beany is a senior member of the club," said Matt. "He does anything we do as long as I'm the president."

"Besides," said Ted, "maybe being small will help. He's harder to see."

"What if no one is there?" said Beany.

"Come back and tell us," said Matt. "Then we'll all go over and look for clues."

"Clues?" said Beany. "What kind of clues?"

"Cut it out, Beany!" said Sam. "Stop talking and go! I'll bet you're scared." He turned to Ted. "He's scared. He's going to talk until it's time to go home."

"We need clues to tell us who they are and what their plans are," said Matt.

"O.K.," said Beany. "I'm ready."

"Good luck," said Matt. He put his hand on Beany's shoulder.

Beany walked away slowly. He didn't look back. Soon he reached the tree house. He looked all around the base of the tree. Nobody was there. He listened. All he could hear was the wind in the leaves. "I'd better look in the tree house," he thought.

Beany climbed up the ladder to the tree house. The ladder creaked each time he took a step. There was a sign on the door. Beany looked at it closely, but he couldn't read it in the dark. Slowly . . . very slowly . . . he pulled the door open. It was pitch black inside.

Then Beany wrapped his shirttail around his flashlight. He turned it on. A soft glow of light filled the room. Beany went in and closed the door after him.

He stepped on a loose board. It came up from the floor at the other end. He saw a piece of paper under the board. "Wow-ee!" whispered Beany. "A clue!"

Beany picked up the paper. There was something written on it in Rusty's handwriting. He read it. "Oh-oh," he thought. "This proves that Rusty and his gang are really against us."

Then he heard a noise. Someone was walking around under the tree. Beany turned off his flashlight.

"I tell you, there's somebody up there," said a voice. "Did you see that light?"

Beany's heart beat faster. That was Rusty's voice, he was sure. Beany tried to swallow, but his throat was dry. He folded the paper and put it back exactly where he'd found it. He shoved the loose board back in place. "Hey!" he heard Rusty say. "You — in the tree house! Come down! You're surrounded. You can't escape!"

For a moment Beany didn't know what to do. Then he remembered the signal. He opened the door and stuck his flashlight out. He turned it on and waved it back and forth.

Suddenly three big bushes around the tree began to shake. Lights flashed on and off.

"What's that?" yelled Rusty. He looked away from the tree house.

"Look out!" someone shouted.

Beany climbed down from the tree house and ran away as fast as he could.

At the Secret Hide-out

Beany ran until he was out of breath. Then he stopped and listened. He heard someone crashing through the bushes ahead of him. He ran away from the noise.

Soon he came to the brook. He stopped and listened again. Everything was quiet.

Beany crossed the brook and walked upstream until he came to the large rock. Then he ran toward the small hill.

At the swampy place he blew his whistle and called his code name: "Red Dragon!"

He waited . . .

"*Beeeeep!* Black Hawk!" it was Matt's voice. "Come into the secret hide-out, Red Dragon."

Beany pushed his way past the tangled grapevines. He entered the secret cave of the Viking Club.

"Hi, Beany," said Matt. "We got here just ahead of you."

Matt, Sam, and Ted were sitting in a circle. Matt's flashlight was turned on. He sat with his back to the entrance of the cave. His hands were partly covering the light. A red glow came through his fingers.

"Boy!" said Beany. "That was a close call. They almost got me." He sat down with his friends.

"That was a great plan Matt had for saving you," said Ted. "It really worked."

"Those guys never even knew it was me," said Beany.

"Did you find any clues?" said Matt.

Beany told them about the paper under the board.

"What did it say? What did it say?" they asked.

"It said Rusty and his gang are going to follow us until they find out where the secret hide-out is," said Beany. "Then they are going to tell everyone where it is."

"That will ruin our club," said Sam.

"Gee, that Rusty sure is mean," said Ted.

"All right, everybody," said Matt. "You've heard Beany's report. We have to stop Rusty and his gang. Does anyone have any ideas?"

"How about sending him a message?" said Beany. "Maybe we could scare him so he wouldn't do it."

"What do you think, Sam?" said Matt.

"I don't think that will work," said Sam.

"I don't either," said Ted. "Rusty's too smart."

Suddenly Sam jumped to his feet. "I got it! I got it!" he yelled.

"Quiet!" said Matt. "Do you want them to hear us?"

"Listen to this!" said Sam. "We have to fool Rusty. We have to *fool* him."

"Fool him?" said Matt. "What do you mean?"

"Well, we know all about their plan," said Sam. "But they don't know that we know it. So we can fool them by leading them to a fake secret hide-out."

"You mean another hide-out?" said Matt.

"Yes," said Sam. "Rusty will tell everyone where it is. We'll make believe he's right. And the real secret hide-out will still be a secret."

"Gee, Sam, you're smart," said Beany. "Will it really work?"

"Sure it'll work," said Matt. "That's a great idea, Sam. What do you think, Ted?"

"It's terrific!" said Ted. "And I know just the right place for a fake secret hide-out."

"Where?" said Matt.

"There's an old chicken coop near my house," said Ted. "There are bushes all around it. Nobody uses it."

"Great," said Matt. "We'll meet under the oak tree tomorrow morning. We'll wait until we see Rusty and his gang hanging around. Then we'll lead them to the chicken coop."

Everybody laughed.

"But remember — don't laugh tomorrow," said Matt, "or Rusty won't believe us."

Capture at the Chicken Coop

THE NEXT MORNING Beany and Ted arrived at the oak tree first. Then they saw Sam coming out of the house.

"Hey, Sam!" said Beany. "Where's Matt?"

"Still in the house," said Sam. He lowered his voice. "He's looking for Rusty from an upstairs window."

The three boys waited for a few minutes.

"Here comes Matt now," said Ted.

"Don't look," said Matt, "but I just saw them behind the bush at the other end of the fence."

"How many are there?" said Ted.

"Three. The same as last night — Rusty, and Larry and Harry Pelton," said Matt. He grinned. "Let's lead them to the chicken coop."

Matt walked away from the boys. Then he said in a loud voice, "Come on, fellows. Let's go to the secret hide-out." He walked fast toward the woods. Sam, Beany, and Ted followed him.

"Are they following us?" said Beany.

"Don't look now," said Matt. "Wait until we get into the woods."

They left the path and walked through tall grasses.

"Where are we going?" said Sam. "This isn't the way to the chicken coop."

"We'll go the long way," said Matt.

Beany sneaked a look over his shoulder.

"Hey! I see them," he said. "They're back where the path turns."

"Good," said Matt. "This is fun. Come on!"

They came to the brook.

"Wait, Matt!" said Sam. "Aren't we going too close to the real secret hide-out?"

"Yeah," said Matt. "Let's walk right past it. I think it's funny. They'll never see it because it's too well hidden."

"You're crazy!" said Beany.

They crossed the brook and found the large stone. Then they walked through the swampy place to the small hill. When they came to the grapevine at the entrance to the secret hide-out, Matt stopped.

"For crying out loud, Matt," whispered Sam. "What are you doing? Don't stop here."

Matt reached up and picked some grapes. He put one in his mouth. "Fooey!" he spit it out. "These wild grapes taste sour." Then he walked past the secret hide-out and over the hill.

They hiked in a half-circle for five minutes. At last they were near the chicken coop.

"Hey, Beany," said Matt. "Are they still behind us?"

Beany turned quickly and looked back down the trail. "Yes," he said. "I can see Rusty's checkered shirt through the trees."

"O.K., fellows," said Matt. "Let's crawl the rest of the way. We have to make it look like a real secret."

"Oh golly!" said Beany. "I hate this part."

The four boys fell flat on the ground. They crawled through weeds and grasses to reach the chicken coop.

"Is everybody in?" said Matt. "Close the door."

"Wait for Beany," said Ted. "He's not such a good crawler."

At last Beany crawled through the doorway. He started laughing as soon as he was inside.

"Sh, Beany," said Matt. "You'll give us away."

"I can't help it," said Beany. He laughed louder.

"Stop it, Beany!" said Sam. "Or I'll sit on you."

"Quiet, fellows," said Matt. "Rusty's hollering something."

"Hey, Vikings!" they heard Rusty yell. "Hey, Vikings! We know where your hide-out is." Then he laughed.

Beany laughed too. "Oh boy!" he said. "This is funny." He couldn't stop laughing. Sam finally sat on him. He held his hand over Beany's mouth.

"What should we do now?" said Ted.

"Let's make believe we're mad at them," said Matt. "Let's chase them away."

"We have them outnumbered," said Beany.

"O.K." said Sam. "Let's go!"

The four members of the Viking Club ran through the doorway of the chicken coop.

"Hey, Rusty!" yelled Sam. "You followed us! You louse!"

"We'll teach you a lesson!" yelled Ted. He shook his fists as he ran.

"Rusty is a sissy!" Beany shouted. "Rusty is a cheater!"

Rusty and his two friends stood still for a moment. They saw Matt, Sam, Beany, and Ted running toward them.

"Let's get out of here!" said Rusty. He ran for the woods. The Pelton twins turned to run after him. Just then Larry Pelton caught his shoe in a tree root.

"I'm stuck! I'm stuck!" he yelled. "Help me! Get me out of here!"

His brother stopped and began tugging at the shoe. "Hey, Rusty!" he shouted. "We have to help Larry."

Rusty stopped running. He looked at his friends. Then he looked at the oncoming Vikings. He turned and ran away as fast as he could.

In a few moments the Vikings surrounded Larry and Harry Pelton.

"You're captured," said Matt.

"Yeah, we know. We give up," said Harry.

"What's the big idea trailing us?" said Matt.

"Aw, Larry and I aren't mad at you guys," said Harry.

"It was Rusty's idea," said Larry.

"And then when we get in trouble, he runs away," said Harry. "Did you see that? We had enough time

to pull Larry free. But Rusty ran away." He shook his head.

"You two are in the wrong club," said Matt. "How would you like to join the Vikings? We always help each other."

"How about it?" said Sam. "How about joining our club?"

"Gee," said Larry Pelton. "Do you really mean it?"

Sam laughed. "Sure we mean it," he said. "We never make jokes."

"Well, hardly ever," said Matt.

"That's right," said Ted.

Beany was laughing so hard he couldn't say anything.